熊俬俬的小吃店 二部曲

文／郭義宏、孟瑛如

圖／林慧婷

英文翻譯／吳侑達

來喲～

登場人物

🐾 松鼠媽媽

🐾 小松鼠

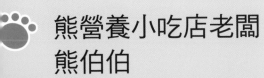

熊營養小吃店老闆
熊伯伯

狼媽媽

小狼

熊伯伯開的小吃店，
生意愈來愈好了。

有一天，熊伯伯發現門口來了兩位新的客人，立刻上前去打招呼。

「兩位好！我是熊伯伯。」熊伯伯說。

狼媽媽微笑說：「你好！這是小狼，我兒子！」

「熊伯伯你好！我聽松鼠媽媽說，你這裡的料理好吃又營養，並且會注重搭配，讓小朋友營養滿滿、頭好壯壯呢！所以今天帶小狼過來看看！」狼媽媽說。

「過獎了！我的餐點其實就是用新鮮的食材加上注意均衡營養成分，也沒有什麼特別的啦！」熊伯伯說。

「也許那就是我們家小狼需要的。」狼媽媽說。

「歡迎你們常常來！」熊伯伯開心的說。

「小狼，你今天想要吃什麼呢？」熊伯伯指著牆上的菜單問。

小狼看了一會兒說：「營養『時』餐是什麼啊？」

「嗯？……我想你說的是營養『特』餐。」熊伯伯愣了一下說。

「不如你今天就吃吃看我的營養特餐吧！」熊伯伯提議。

「那裡面有什麼呢？」小狼問。

「你吃吃看就知道囉！」熊伯伯說：「不過，你敢吃牡蠣嗎？」

「牡蠣？敢吃啊！」小狼大聲說。

「太好了！你們先請坐，一下就好了。」熊伯伯說。

來喲～

過了一會兒，熊伯伯端了一個托盤出來。

「來，這是今天的營養特餐——牡蠣披薩加鮮蚵豆腐湯。」

「牡蠣披薩？我還是第一次見到這樣的披薩，真特別！」
狼媽媽說。

「沒什麼，只是把食材做不同的組合而已。」熊伯伯說。

「國字也是一樣喔！」熊伯伯轉身對小狼說：「就像我把食材做不同的搭配一樣，不同的部首和部件，就會組合出不同的字。」

「嗯！」小狼迫不及待的塞了滿嘴食物，一邊回答著。

這時候，小松鼠和松鼠媽媽正好從門外進來。

「嗨！小狼，你們也來了？」

小松鼠很快的走到小狼旁邊說：「你已經在吃了？你點了什麼？好吃嗎？很好吃對不對？」小松鼠一口氣連連追問，小狼根本來不及回答。

「嗯！好吃！我點了營養特餐，是牡蠣披薩加鮮蚵豆腐湯。」小狼說。

「牡蠣嗎？以前我不愛吃，可是熊伯伯說這很營養，而且他煮得很好吃，對不對？」小松鼠開心的說。

「你要不要吃？我們一起吃吧！」小狼說。

「好啊！」小松鼠高興的說。

小狼和小松鼠一起愉快的吃著營養特餐。

松鼠媽媽對狼媽媽說：「小狼真是會分享呢！」

「他是挺貼心的沒錯，可是學習上就很傷腦筋……」狼媽媽憂心的說：「老師說他的閱讀和寫字能力都有點兒落後。」

「學習上的困難，學校老師會幫他想辦法。」熊伯伯說：
「媽媽妳可以照顧好他的營養均衡和睡眠，讓他有充足的元
氣去學習。」

「小朋友的成長過程一定要均衡的攝取各類食物，才能有足夠的營養。」熊伯伯接著說。

「嗯！謝謝你，我會幫他多注意。」狼媽媽說。

食物金字塔

脂肪、油和甜食

牛奶、優酪乳和起司

肉、魚、豆類蛋、乾果

蔬菜

水果

麵包、麥片、米飯和麵類

「而且，」熊伯伯繼續說：「食物裡的許多營養素，如：維生素 B6、葉酸、鎂、鋅、DHA 和 EPA 等，都可以提升小狼的學習能力喔！今天的牡蠣披薩加鮮蚵豆腐湯就含豐富的鋅呢！」

「是嗎？那真是太好了！」狼媽媽說。

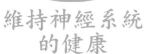

維持神經系統
的健康

葉酸

輔助神經細胞
代謝

鎂

維持神經
和肌肉健康

DHA、EPA

提升大腦學習
及記憶功能

鋅

加強記憶功能
和反應能力

「是啊，我們小松鼠以前的學習和行為表現，也是讓我傷透腦筋。」松鼠媽媽說：「後來從熊伯伯這裡學到了良好的飲食習慣，現在他的表現令人放心多了！」

「那我們以後常常跟你們一起來好嗎？」狼媽媽興奮的說。

「對了！」松鼠媽媽說：「我幫小松鼠報名了熊伯伯的『營養小廚師』班，要不要讓小狼也來參加？」

「讓小狼來學做菜嗎？」狼媽媽有點訝異的說。

「是啊！讓他們多參加一些活動，可以增加他們的生活經驗。」松鼠媽媽說。

「嗯！我想提供一些讓小朋友可以『動手做』的機會，讓他們能夠發展得更好。」熊伯伯說。

「那我問問看小狼吧！」狼媽媽說。

「我要！我要！」小狼在旁邊興奮的跳來跳去說：「我想要參加！」

「你聽見我們說的啦？……那你就跟小松鼠一起來上課吧！」
狼媽媽說。

「YA!」小狼和小松鼠齊聲歡呼。

給教師及家長的話

　　自從《熊伯伯的小吃店》繪本在 2016 年出版以來，有趣的故事、活潑的繪圖，以及針對親子可一起動手做的簡單美味食譜，讓這本繪本廣受好評，更名列臺北市推動兒童深耕閱讀工作計畫 105 年度「兒童閱讀優良媒材」圖書類一到三年級優良推薦書單中，這給了我們有愛無礙研究團隊很大的鼓舞！尤其在陳述注重營養均衡，食用含維生素 B6、葉酸、Omega-3、高蛋白等營養成分的食物可改善孩子的注意力及衝動行為後，有愛無礙網站上所整理的應用膳食療養概念（亦即融合基礎的食物學、營養學與生理、生化等科學的概念，了解各種營養評估與膳食介入之原則），似乎更能廣受大家喜愛。運用繪本方式也讓健康飲食習慣在孩子心中成形，學會從小善待自己的身體。

　　繪本在教學上的應用本就是巧妙各自不同，例如一位國小校長運用《熊伯伯的小吃店》在晨讀時朗讀給低年級孩子聽，主要用意是希望能改善孩子不愛吃青菜的習慣。當她提及進行完這個活動後，低年級老師們回報連續兩週營養午餐的青菜筒都空空如也時，校長因成就感而微笑發光的臉，是筆者至今每次提筆想要創作新繪本時最大的動力來源！

　　《熊伯伯的小吃店》中的營養膳食主要是針對有注意力缺陷過動行為的孩子來設計的，而在教學現場，有學習困難、記憶力不佳的孩子其實更多，哪些食物可以為腦袋加分呢？許多營養師均推薦含鋅和鎂的食物，最主要是因鋅對腦部的功能運作有非常重要的地位。鋅在人體內形同一位高超的指揮家，它指導及監督身體的各種活動，並保持人體中細胞及酵素的正常功能，可以讓身體內各項活動協調運作。如果鋅的攝取量不足，就容易出現記憶力衰退、注意力不集中的問題。牡蠣、全穀類、核果類中鋅的含量非常豐富，另外，肝臟、牛肉、蟹、乳製品、豆類等亦是不錯的來源。而鎂則是人體不可缺少的礦物質之一，具有維持神經和肌肉健康，保護骨骼和平衡血糖的重要作用。現代人之所以容易產生鎂攝取不足的問題，主要是因為多數人吃的是容易導致鎂離子流失的高度加工精煉食物；然而鎂是葉綠素中的主要成分，因此鎂多存在於富含葉綠素的蔬菜中，吃多種蔬菜、水果和全穀物，將有助於攝取足夠的鎂！根據維基百科的資料，紫菜含鎂量最高，每 100 克紫菜中含鎂 460 毫克。

　　《熊伯伯的小吃店～二部曲》因此誕生！故事中端出牡蠣披薩加鮮蚵豆腐湯等創意料理，並且在每道料理的繪圖都加上很多綠意，希望能提醒孩子多吃蔬菜、水果，補充鋅和鎂。另外，在閱讀本繪本時，也別忘了提醒孩子要多吃以下幾類食物幫腦袋加分喔！

1. 深色水果及富含維生素C的蔬果：深色水果如藍莓、葡萄、櫻桃及草莓等莓類，這些深色水果中所含的強力抗氧化物，對於減緩老化、活化腦力和增強記憶力有相當幫助。而腦細胞需要維生素 C 的抗氧化功能來免於自由基破壞，所以富含維生素C的蔬果也可以多吃喔！例如：葡萄柚、番石榴、柳丁、番茄、奇異果、花椰菜等。

2. 含豐富 Omega-3 脂肪酸的魚類：例如鮪魚、鮭魚、鯖魚、沙丁魚或秋刀魚等。Omega-3 脂肪酸可維持大腦神經傳導功能正常運作，幫助腦部細胞運送營養並清除廢物。

3. 全穀類食物：營養學界一直大力推薦富含維生素 E 及維生素 B1、葉酸、菸鹼酸等的全穀類食物，其所含的營養成分全都是維持正常大腦機能必要的營養素，像是全麥麵包、糙米、麥片等都是好選擇。

4. 卡通人物大力水手卜派最愛的菠菜：菠菜裡含有大量維生素 C、E 及 β 蘿蔔素等抗氧化物質，可以保護腦細胞不受自由基損害，維持大腦的年輕活力，所以除了大力水手吃了會力大無比外，更有人稱菠菜為蔬菜之王呢！在臺灣，如果是平地菠菜與高山菠菜輪替，就幾乎一年四季都可吃到，是一種幸福的滋味！

5. 各類堅果：這也是營養學界一直大力推薦的食物，因為堅果中富含單元不飽和脂肪，有降低膽固醇的功能，其所含的礦物質──硼，能夠影響腦部的電流活動，使人的反應變得更靈敏，而且還有豐富的維生素E、硒等抗氧化物質，可以保護腦細胞不受到自由基的損害。

6. 富含 β 蘿蔔素食物：β 蘿蔔素這種抗氧化物質能幫助我們擁有健康年輕的腦力，維持較敏銳的思考能力。南瓜、南瓜子、胡蘿蔔、甜椒、番薯、木瓜等都富含 β 蘿蔔素。

7. 雞蛋：蛋黃中富含的卵磷脂，是人體合成大腦中負責記憶力的神經傳導物質之主要原料。舉凡簡單的水煮蛋、荷包蛋、蒸蛋、滷蛋、炒蛋等，大都是小朋友的最愛，每天一至兩顆蛋是可以接受的量。

最後，建議以上的食物盡可能是簡單處理即可上桌，以能吃到食物的原來形態為主，千萬別為了求美味而過度加工，或烹調至營養成分盡失。通常也較不鼓勵以市售的包裝健康食品取代天然食物，畢竟天然食物是上帝造的，包裝的健康食品卻是人造的！

熊伯伯食譜

牡蠣披薩

材料

牡蠣、墨西哥餅皮、綠花椰菜、沙拉醬、起司絲

步驟

1. 綠花椰菜切一口大小，洗乾淨後放入滾水中滾煮約 1 分鐘，撈起瀝乾。

2. 牡蠣洗淨，置入滾水中汆燙至再次滾開，撈起瀝乾。

3. 墨西哥餅皮抹上沙拉醬，將牡蠣及綠花椰菜排列其上，撒上起司絲。

4. 烤箱溫度設定 200 度，預熱後將披薩置入烤 10 分鐘。

5. 取出後切片，撒上義式香料即完成。

小秘訣

1. 牡蠣加熱過程會釋出水分，所以要先汆燙瀝乾，避免水分太多影響口感。

2. 墨西哥餅皮可用其他的餅皮代替，如蛋餅皮、吐司麵包或蔥油餅等等。沙拉醬也可以用番茄醬、烤肉醬、咖哩醬等等醬料替換，在家就能做出各種口味的披薩。

3. 清洗牡蠣時，建議逐一摸過牡蠣脣，較容易找到並去除殘留的牡蠣殼。

鮮蚵豆腐湯

材料

牡蠣、豆腐、酸菜、嫩薑、蔥

步驟

1. 牡蠣洗淨,豆腐及酸菜切一口大小,蔥切段、薑切片數片。

2. 取適量水,水滾後置入所有材料,煮至再次水滾開。

3. 熄火,加鹽、胡椒、香油調味即完成。

小祕訣

1. 小朋友通常不喜歡湯裡有薑絲、蔥花、香菜等細碎的辛香料,家長可以將辛香料切片或切段,方便小朋友盛裝時避開。

2. 若牡蠣新鮮度稍差,則可將牡蠣另鍋汆燙好再加到湯裡,以去除腥味。

海鮮蒸蛋

材料

蛋 3 顆、蝦仁、牡蠣、蛤蜊、小卷等海鮮

步驟

1. 海鮮洗淨後切一口大小，置入滾水中汆燙至再次滾開，撈起放涼。

2. 蛋打勻，汆燙海鮮的水放涼，加 3 杯（量米杯，約 150 毫升／杯）於蛋液中，加少許鹽後攪拌均勻。

3. 放入海鮮，水滾入鍋蒸 15 分鐘即完成。

小秘訣

1. 海鮮須先燙過，以免在蒸蛋中有未熟之虞。汆燙海鮮的水放涼後，可以作為高湯，增加蒸蛋的鮮味。

2. 1 顆蛋加約 150 毫升的高湯或水，可以蒸出軟嫩的蒸蛋。

3. 蒸蛋時，不要將鍋蓋蓋緊，在鍋蓋下架一根筷子或是將鍋蓋斜一邊，可以讓蒸蛋表面光滑好看。

嫩煎牛排

材料

牛排

步驟

1. 前一日將冷凍牛排置於冷藏，使之完全解凍。

2. 取出牛排，於兩面撒上少許鹽。

3. 鍋中加熱少許油，牛排入鍋，中大火煎烤，每 20～30 秒翻面一次，煎至表面微焦。

4. 盛盤靜置 2 分鐘以上，盤中會有少許血水，換一個乾淨的盤子即完成。

小秘訣

1. 將牛排置於冷藏解凍時，不需包覆塑膠袋或保鮮膜，冰箱的空氣能讓牛排表面保持乾燥，達到熟成的效果。

2. 不斷翻面，可以避免牛排內部過熟過老。反之，煎魚則要減少翻面的次數，魚才容易熟透。

3. 剛加熱好的肉，裡面的肉汁呈游離狀態，切起來會有較多血水。稍微靜置後，肉汁會鎖回肉裡，成為軟嫩多汁的牛排，且切起來不太會有血水。

涼拌海帶芽

材料

海帶芽、洋蔥

步驟

1. 乾的海帶芽泡水，洋蔥切絲。
2. 將海帶芽及洋蔥絲放入滾水中，滾煮約 2 分鐘後瀝乾放涼。
3. 加入香油及鰹魚醬油，拌勻即完成。

小祕訣

1. 若是成人要食用，可以用生洋蔥涼拌，並加入薑絲、蒜末及烏醋，以增添風味。
2. 如果沒有鰹魚醬油或淡醬油，可以用糖和鹽代替，若加一般醬油，恐怕會有過重的醬油味。

Uncle Bear's Eatery: Meet Mama Wolf and Little Wolf

Written by Yi-Hung Kuo &
Ying-Ru Meng
Illustrated by Hui-Ting Lin
Translated by Arik Wu

Characters

The boss of "Beary" Yummy Uncle Bear

Mama Squirrel

Little Squirrel

Mama Wolf

Little Wolf

Since the visits of Mama Squirrel and Little Squirrel, Uncle Bear's eatery had become more and more popular.

One day, Uncle Bear saw two customers approaching the doorway of the eatery. He immediately went over to greet them.

"Hello there! I'm Uncle Bear," he said.

"Hi! This is my son, Little Wolf," Mama Wolf said with a smile on her face.

"Nice to meet you, Uncle Bear! I've heard from Mama Squirrel that the foods here are very delicious and nutritious. I think they will be very beneficial for wolf cubs. So I figured it might be a good idea to take Little Wolf here for a meal or two," Mama Wolf said.

"Ah, thank you! I'm flattered indeed. All I do is pay a little more attention to the freshness of the ingredients I use to make food. You know, to make sure that they're nutritious. It's no big deal actually," Uncle Bear said.

"Maybe that's just what my son needs the most," Mama Wolf said.

"You're welcome to come around any time!" Uncle Bear seemed pleased.

"What'd you love to eat today, Little Wolf?" Uncle Bear asked, pointing to the menu on the wall.

"What exactly is 'Specially *Nutriment* Meal'?" Little Wolf stared at the menu for a short while and asked.

Uncle Bear paused, seemingly baffled. "Do you mean 'Specially *Nutritious* Meal'?" he asked.

"Anyway, why not give it a try?" Uncle Bear suggested.

"But I have no idea what it is!" Little Wolf said.

"Well, you'll know if you give it a try. I hope you have no problem with oysters, though," Uncle Bear said.

"Oysters? Of course not!" Little Wolf said.

"Ok then. Please be seated. Your meal will be served in no time," Uncle Bear said.

Shortly afterward, Uncle Bear came in with a tray of food. "This is today's Specially Nutritious Meal—Oyster Pizza and Oyster Tofu Soup!" said Uncle Bear.

"Oyster Pizza? How special! This is something new to me," Mama Wolf said.

"Just mixing up different recipes. It's no big deal," Uncle Bear said.

"By the way," Uncle Bear turned around, and talked to Little Wolf. "Just as there're ways of dealing with different foods, there're also ways of arranging letters to make different words. Prefixes and suffixes, you know."

"Got it!" Little Wolf said while munching the food before him.

This was when Mama Squirrel and Little Squirrel came in through the door.

"Hey, I didn't know you were here already, Little Wolf," Little Squirrel said. "What are you eating? What did you order? Is it yummy? I bet it is. I bet it is! RIGHT?"

Little Squirrel talked way too fast that Little Wolf could not answer his questions right away.

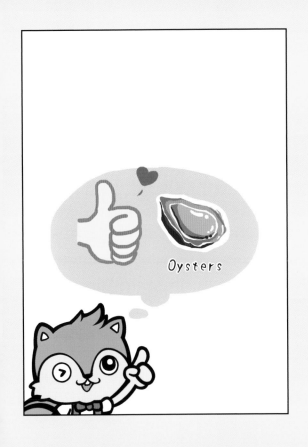

"Yeah, it's pretty good. I ordered today's Specially Nutritious Meal—Oyster Pizza and Oyster Tofu Soup," said Little Wolf.

"Oysters? They weren't my favorite, but since Uncle Bear knows how to cook them to perfection and he told me once they are rich in protein and minerals, I love them now!" Little Squirrel said.

"Would you like some? We can share!" Little Wolf said.

"Sure. Thanks!" Little Squirrel said happily. Little Wolf and Little Squirrel enjoyed the meal together. They both seemed really happy.

"It seems like your son is really kind and caring," Mama Squirrel said to Mama Wolf.

"Indeed he is. He is a very sweet kid. The problem is that he kind of falls behind in his schoolwork. His teacher said his reading and handwriting abilities are not on the same level as his peers," Mama Wolf said worriedly.

"Well, I'm sure his teacher will help him catch up with schoolwork. All you need to do is make sure that he has enough sleep and nutrition. Otherwise he'll not have the energy to study even if his teacher tries to help out," Uncle Bear said.

"If you want Little Wolf to grow up healthy and strong, you've got to give him balanced diets, " Uncle Bear continued.

"Thanks for your advice! I'll make sure he's well-fed," Mama Wolf said.

"Incidentally," Uncle Bear continued. "A lot of the nutrients in foods, such as Vitamin B6, folate, magnesium, zinc, DHA*, and EPA**, can help Little Wolf learn faster and remember better. Oyster pizza and oyster tofu soup, for example, contain a high proportion of zinc!"

"Really? That's fantastic!" Mama Wolf said.

*DHA = Docosahexaenoic Acid

**EPA = Eicosapentaenoic Acid

"Back then, I was really worried about Little Squirrel's academic performance and his behavior, to be frank," Mama Squirrel said. "But now that he maintains a healthy, regular diet, I certainly feel much more relaxed. We thank Uncle Bear for that."

"Awesome! Do you think we can join you in visiting Uncle Bear in the future?" Mama Wolf said in excitement.

"Sure! I just enrolled Little Squirrel in Uncle Bear's *Little Chef* class, where he'll get to learn some basic cooking techniques. Do you think Little Wolf will be interested?" Mama Squirrel asked.

"You think it's a good idea to have my son learn how to cook?" Mama Wolf seemed a bit surprised.

"I do. I think it helps to participate in some more activities. You know, it allows the young ones to explore different aspects of life," Mama Squirrel said.

"Exactly. I want to better develop our young friends' potentials by providing them with some hands-on experiences," Uncle Bear added.